# Hairy Maclary Scattercat

## Lynley Dodd

Spindlewood

Hairy Maclary
felt bumptious and bustly,
bossy and bouncy
and frisky and hustly.
He wanted to run.
He wanted to race.
But the MAIN thing he wanted
was something
to
chase.

Greywacke Jones
was hunting a bee.

BUT ALONG CAME HAIRY MACLARY. . .

and chased her up high
in the sycamore tree.

Butterball Brown
was washing a paw.

BUT ALONG CAME HAIRY MACLARY. . .

and bustled him under
a rickety door.

Pimpernel Pugh
was patting a ball.

BUT ALONG CAME HAIRY MACLARY. . .

and chased her away
over Pemberton's wall.

Slinky Malinki
was down in the reeds.

BUT ALONG CAME HAIRY MACLARY. . .

and hustled him into
a drum full of weeds.

Mushroom Magee
was asleep on a ledge.

BUT ALONG CAME HAIRY MACLARY. . .

and chased her away
through a hole in the hedge.

Down on the path
by an old wooden rail,
twitching a bit,
was the tip of a tail.
With a bellicose bark
and a boisterous bounce,
Hairy Maclary
was ready
to
POUNCE

BUT AROUND CAME SCARFACE CLAW...

who bothered
and bustled him,
rustled and hustled him,
raced him
and chased him

ALL the way
home.

British Library Cataloguing in Publication Data
Dodd, Lynley
    Hairy Maclary Scattercat
    1.  Title
    823[J] PZ7

**Other Lynley Dodd books**

MY CAT LIKES TO HIDE IN BOXES (with Eve Sutton)
THE NICKLE NACKLE TREE
TITIMUS TRIM
THE APPLE TREE
THE SMALLEST TURTLE
HAIRY MACLARY FROM DONALDSON'S DAIRY
HAIRY MACLARY'S BONE

Published in 1985 by Spindlewood
70 Lynhurst Avenue, Barnstaple, Devon EX31 2HY.

First published in 1985 by
Mallinson Rendel Publishers Ltd.
Wellington, New Zealand.

Reprinted in September 1985
Reprinted March 1990
© Lynley Dodd, 1985

ISBN 0-907349-46-3

Printed and bound by Colorcraft Ltd., Hong Kong.